Table of Contents

Rourke
Educational Media
rourkeeducationalmedia.com

Can you find these words?

crown

Harbor

Statue

torch

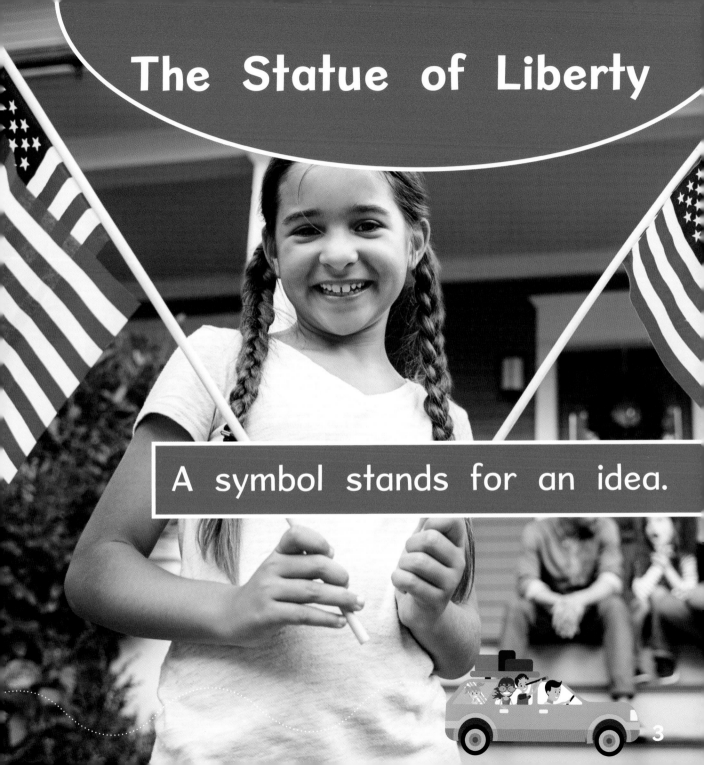

The Statue of Liberty

A symbol stands for an idea.

The **Statue** of Liberty is a symbol of freedom.

Liberty means to be free.

The statue is in New York **Harbor.**

It welcomes people to the United States.

Its **torch** is a symbol of light and knowledge.

Its book is a symbol of laws.

The **crown** has seven points.

The world has seven continents.

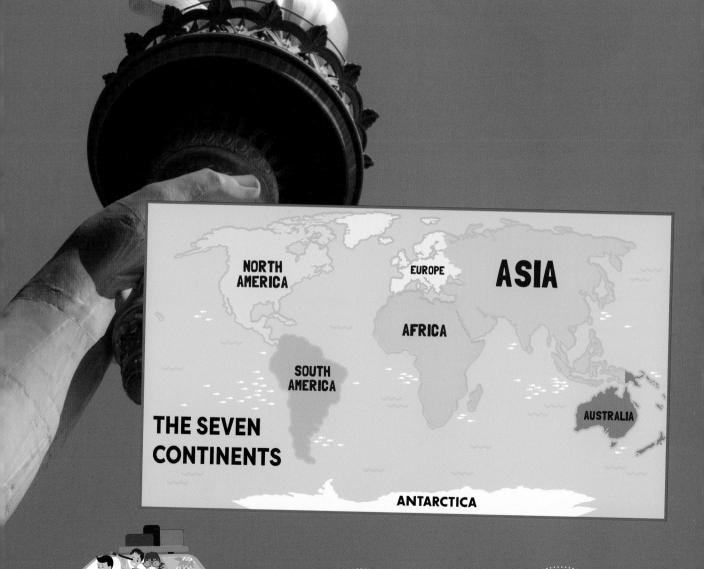

THE SEVEN CONTINENTS

NORTH AMERICA
SOUTH AMERICA
EUROPE
AFRICA
ASIA
AUSTRALIA
ANTARCTICA

Liberty is for everyone, everywhere.

Did you find these words?

The **crown** has seven points.

The statue is in New York **Harbor**.

The **Statue** of Liberty is a symbol of freedom.

Its **torch** is a symbol of light and knowledge.

Photo Glossary

 **crown** (kroun): A headdress often worn by queens and kings.

 **harbor** (HAHR-bur): An area of calm water near land, often a place where ships can dock or anchor safely.

 **statue** (STACH-oo): A model of a person or an animal made from metal, stone, or other materials.

 **torch** (torch): A flaming light that can be carried.

Index

About the Author

K.A. Robertson is a writer and editor who enjoys learning about the history of the United States. She's visited the Statue of Liberty many times. She has even climbed the stairs inside to the top of the crown!

www.rourkeeducationalmedia.com

PHOTO CREDITS: Cover: ©TriggerPhoto; p2,10,14,15: ©GBlakeley; p2,6,14,15: ©GCShutter; p2,4,14,15: ©franckreporter; p2,8,14,15: ©evenfh; p3: ©monkeybusinessimages; p9: ©wilson7914; p11: ©KanKhem; p12: ©Joshua Haviv; p12: ©M_a_y_a

Edited by: Keli Sipperley

Cover and interior design by: Rhea Magaro-Wallace

Library of Congress PCN Data
Statue of Liberty / K.A. Robertson
(Visiting U.S. Symbols)
ISBN 978-1-64369-056-8 (hard cover)(alk. paper)
ISBN 978-1-64369-082-7 (soft cover)
ISBN 978-1-64369-203-6 (e-Book)
Library of Congress Control Number: 2018955827

Printed in the United States of America, North Mankato, Minnesota